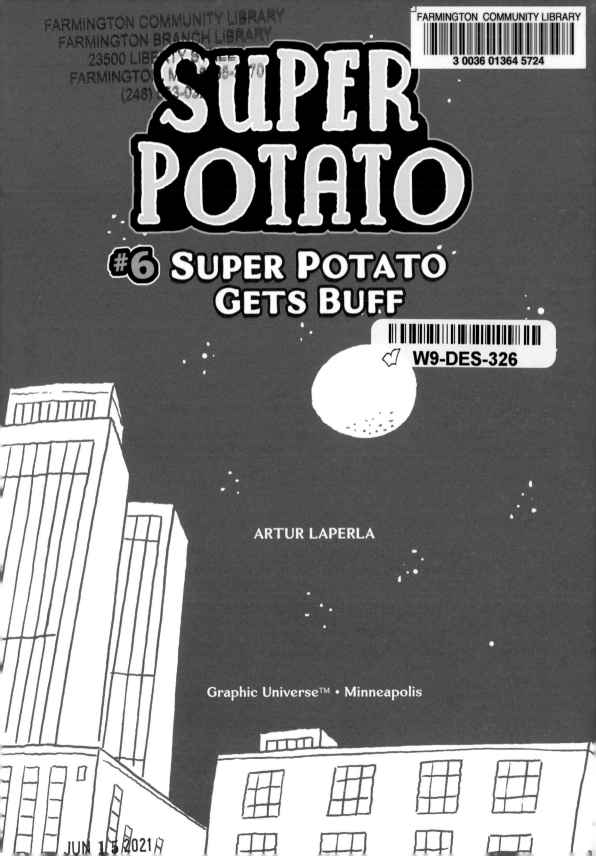

SUPER POTATO

#6 SUPER POTATO GETS BUFF

ARTUR LAPERLA

Graphic Universe™ • Minneapolis

Story and illustrations by Artur Laperla
Translation by Norwyn MacTíre

First American edition published in 2021 by Graphic Universe™

Graphic Universe™
An imprint of Lerner Publishing Group, Inc.
241 First Avenue North
Minneapolis, MN 55401 USA

For reading levels and more information, look up this title at www.lernerbooks.com.

Main body text set in CCWildWords. Typeface provided by Comicraft.

Library of Congress Cataloging-in-Publication Data

Names: Laperla (Artist), author, illustrator. | MacTire, Norwyn, translator.
Title: Super Potato gets buff / Artur Laperla ; translation by Norwyn MacTíre.
Other titles: Super Patata. 6. English
Description: First American edition. | Minneapolis, MN : Graphic Universe, 2021. | Series: Super Potato book 6 | Audience: Ages 7–11 | Audience: Grades 2–3 | Summary: "Gigantic flies are rampaging at a research center, thanks to a beam that boosted their molecules! Fortunately, the beam also creates a gigantic Super Potato . . . who's delighted with his new muscles" —Provided by publisher.
Identifiers: LCCN 2020006429 (print) | LCCN 2020006430 (ebook) | ISBN 9781512440263 (library binding) | ISBN 9781728417523 (ebook)
Subjects: LCSH: Graphic novels. | CYAC: Graphic novels. | Superheroes—Fiction. | Potatoes—Fiction. | Humorous stories.
Classification: LCC PZ7.7.L367 Sv 2020 (print) | LCC PZ7.7.L367 (ebook) | DDC 741.5/973—dc23

LC record available at https://lccn.loc.gov/2020006429
LC ebook record available at https://lccn.loc.gov/2020006430

Manufactured in the United States of America
1-42295-26145-6/10/2020

4

SUPER POTATO ARRIVES AT THE CORTEX RESEARCH SECTORS . . .

THAT'S A LOT OF BUZZING!

THANK YOU FOR COMING, MISTER POTATO!

SUPER POTATO!

ALLOW ME TO PRESENT MY COLLEAGUE PROFESSOR MOLECULE. TOGETHER WE'LL EXPLAIN WHAT HAPPENED . . .

IT'S ALL MY FAULT!

LET'S TAKE A QUICK BREAK FROM ALL THAT BUZZING AND SHOUTING. HERE'S A NICE LITTLE DIAGRAM TO EXPLAIN THE SITUATION:

PROFESSOR MOLECULE WORKS ON TWO DIFFERENT TYPES OF BEAMS*.

THE RED BEAM ACCELERATES MOLECULAR GROWTH.

THE GREEN BEAM ACCELERATES MOLECULAR REDUCTION.

BY ACCIDENT (OR THROUGH THE SHEER INCOMPETENCE OF PROFESSOR MOLECULE), THREE FLIES HE HAD TREATED WITH THE RED BEAM BROKE FREE WITHIN HIS SECTOR.

I DON'T KNOW HOW IT HAPPENED!

*SCIENTISTS LOVE THEIR FANCY BEAMS.

SUPER POTATO HAS FOUGHT ALL KINDS OF PESTS, BUT IT'S STILL A BIT OF A SHOCK TO MEET A GIANT FLY.

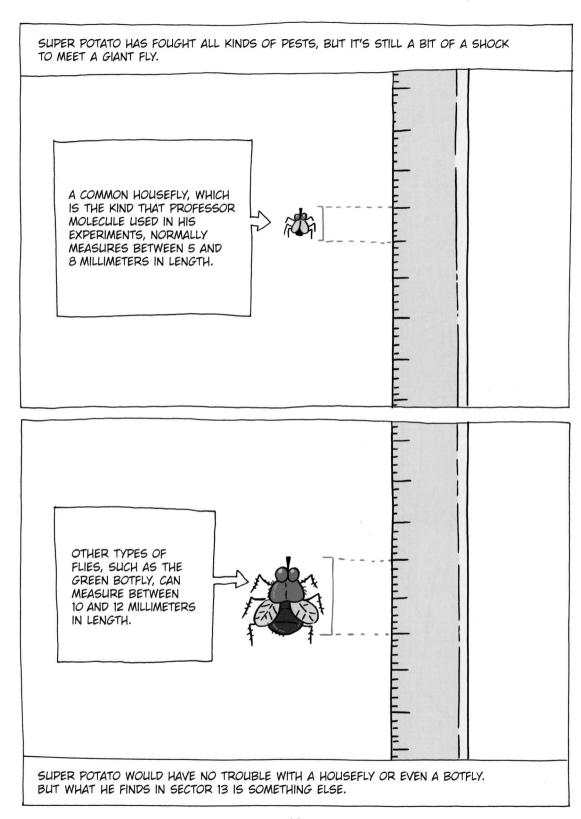

A COMMON HOUSEFLY, WHICH IS THE KIND THAT PROFESSOR MOLECULE USED IN HIS EXPERIMENTS, NORMALLY MEASURES BETWEEN 5 AND 8 MILLIMETERS IN LENGTH.

OTHER TYPES OF FLIES, SUCH AS THE GREEN BOTFLY, CAN MEASURE BETWEEN 10 AND 12 MILLIMETERS IN LENGTH.

SUPER POTATO WOULD HAVE NO TROUBLE WITH A HOUSEFLY OR EVEN A BOTFLY. BUT WHAT HE FINDS IN SECTOR 13 IS SOMETHING ELSE.

BUT CATCHING FLIES ISN'T EASY, EVEN WHEN THEY'RE REALLY, REALLY BIG.

IT STOPPED! I'LL GRAB THAT ONE . . .

BZT

THANKS TO ITS SOPHISTICATED DEFENSE SYSTEM, A FLY CAN ANTICIPATE SUPER POTATO'S EVERY MOVE!

HEY! DON'T GO!

PFFF!

IT'S HARDER THAN
I THOUGHT!

THIS HAPPENS
A LOT.

LUCKILY, SUPER POTATO KNOWS THE
BEST TOOLS FOR HUNTING FLIES ARE
PATIENCE . . .

HMMM . . .

. . . GOOD REFLEXES . . .

. . . AND SUPER SPEED.

NOW!

THE PROBLEM IS THAT WHILE SUPER POTATO PREPARES TO FACE THE SECOND FLY . . .

PHASE ONE: PATIENCE

. . . THE FIRST FLY . . .

BZT

BZZZZZZ

. . . REVIVES ITSELF.

AND WHEN THE SECOND ONE FINALLY DROPS . . .

. . . TWO OTHER FLIES ARE STILL FLUTTERING AROUND.

NOT AS MUCH PATIENCE

GRRRR!

23

*TO RECALL THE MINOR DIFFERENCES, FLIP BACK TO PAGE 7

26

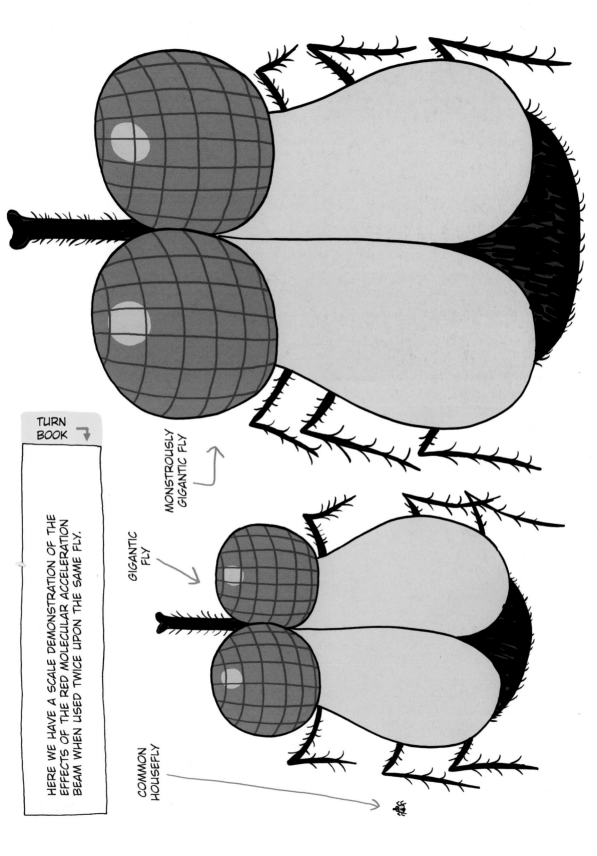

TURN
BOOK ↳

HERE WE HAVE A SCALE DEMONSTRATION OF THE EFFECTS OF THE RED MOLECULAR ACCELERATION BEAM WHEN USED TWICE UPON THE SAME FLY.

MONSTROUSLY GIGANTIC FLY

GIGANTIC FLY

COMMON HOUSEFLY

IN A MATTER OF SECONDS, THE GIGANTIC FLY . . .

. . . HAS BECOME A MONSTROUS ONE, AND IT'S READY TO TAKE FLIGHT.

AT THIS POINT, IT'S IMPORTANT
TO PAUSE FOR A MOMENT.
WHAT'S ABOUT TO HAPPEN IS
BEST EXPLAINED STEP-BY-STEP:

SUPER POTATO
FLIES TO GRAB
THE REDUCTION
BEAM . . .

BUT THE MONSTER FLY
IS SO BIG . . .

. . . IT CAN'T EVEN SUPPORT
ITS OWN WEIGHT . . .

34

35

AND BECAUSE PROBLEMS NEVER COME ONE AT A TIME, JUST AS SUPER POTATO STARTS FEELING THE EFFECTS OF THE RED BEAM...

. . . THE OTHER GIANT FLIES PERK UP.

37

41

. . . I'M AFRAID THE RED BEAM HAS ALSO AFFECTED MISTER POTATO.

THE RESULT IS MOST UNUSUAL. PERHAPS BECAUSE OF HIS BODY'S GENETIC MIXTURE OF HUMAN-SUPERHERO CELLS AND POTATO CELLS.

THE BEAM! GRRFFF!

HERE IT IS!! HOLD ON, SUPER POTATO!

RRRRR

A CASE WORTHY OF MUCH STUDY . . .

43

AND SO . . .

GET OUT OF HERE!

WELL, THE BEAMS WORK WONDERFULLY ON FLIES . . .

GO OUTSIDE!

. . . AND THEIR EFFECT ON MISTER SUPER POTATO IS RATHER INTERESTING AS WELL.

UH . . .

IF SMOKE LEADS YOU TO A FIRE, LOUD BUZZING LEADS YOU TO GIANT FLIES.

48

THE UNFORTUNATE FACT ABOUT HUNTING FLIES IS THAT . . .

GET OVER HERE!

. . . EVEN NOW, IT'S NOT VERY EASY.

DID YOU HEAR ME!? COME HERE!

IT DOESN'T MATTER IF THE PERSON DOING THE HUNTING IS SUPER POTATO . . .

AND STOP BUZZING!!

. . . OR **SUPER** SUPER POTATO.

GRRRR!

PUFFING HIS CHEST

HMPH! I'M A TINY BIT FED UP WITH THESE FLIES!

SUDDENLY . . .

SHH BLAM

BZZZT

HUH!?

TAKE THAT!

HA! ONE FLY DOWN.

WAIT A SEC, IT'S . . .

*IF YOU'VE READ **SUPER POTATO'S MEGA TIME-TRAVEL ADVENTURE** AND **SUPER POTATO AND THE MUTANT ANIMAL MAYHEM**, YOU KNOW THAT SUPER POTATO HAS A LITTLE CRUSH ON HER.

53

HUH? OH, NO, THIS IS A VISITOR'S PASS. AND THE LAB COAT'S A LOANER.

I'VE COME TO SEE A FRIEND...

WHO COULD IT BE?

LET'S TAKE THIS PART STEP-BY-STEP TOO. OLIVIA OLSON IS A MARINE BIOLOGIST. SHE WORKS AT THE CITY AQUARIUM.

SHE'S VISITING THE CORTEX CENTER FOR ULTRA-ADVANCED RESEARCH ALONGSIDE GLADYS, THE SMARTEST DOLPHIN IN THE AQUARIUM. IN THE WHOLE WORLD, PROBABLY.

GLADYS ASSISTS VARIOUS SCIENTISTS IN SOLVING COMPLEX MATHEMATICAL EQUATIONS.

EEEEEE.

EEEEE.

ARE YOU SURE?

WHEW!

WELL, IT SEEMS AS IF OLIVIA OLSON HAS FINALLY BROUGHT AN END TO THE THREAT OF THE GIGANTIC FLIES. SUPER POTATO JUST HAS TO DRAG THEM OVER TO PROFESSOR MOLECULE AND THE GREEN REDUCTION BEAM.

THAT BUZZING WAS DRIVING ME NUTS!

WHERE DID THESE BIG FLIES COME FROM?

REALLY WEIRD TO SEE YOU, BY THE WAY . . .

MMFF!

AND SO, ONCE AGAIN, WE INEVITABLY ARRIVE AT THE FINAL PAGE. THE GIGANTIC FLIES WILL RETURN TO THEIR REGULAR SIZE. AND SUPER POTATO . . . WHAT CAN WE SAY ABOUT SUPER POTATO? WHAT WILL HAPPEN WITH ALL THOSE MUSCLES? GOOD QUESTION! BUT . . .

I DON'T LOOK HALF BAD. NOT BAD AT ALL . . .

THE END

. . . AS THEY SAY, THE REST IS HISTORY. UNTIL THE NEXT ADVENTURE!

For more hilarious tales of Super Potato, check out . . .

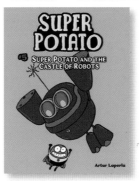

AND TURN THE PAGE FOR A PREVIEW OF OUR HERO'S NEXT GREAT ADVENTURE . . .